ILLUSTRATORS

Tom LaPadula—*Noah's Ark*
Moses in the Bulrushes
David and Goliath
The Lord Is My Shepherd
Daniel in the Lions' Den

Pamela Ford Johnson—*Joseph and the Coat of Many Colors*

Roberta Collier—*The Story of Jonah*

Tony Chen—Cover illustration

Two-Minute Bible Stories

Old Testament Favorites, Including *Noah's Ark*, *Moses in the Bulrushes*, and *David and Goliath*

Retold by Pamela Broughton

A GOLDEN BOOK • NEW YORK

Western Publishing Company, Inc., Racine, Wisconsin 53404

Noah's Ark

The people of the world had become very wicked. God found only one good person in all the world, a man named Noah.

God said to Noah, "I will bring a flood upon the earth. Everything will die." God told Noah to build an ark of wood and to cover it with tar, inside and out.

"In the ark, you and your family will be safe from the flood. Bring along two of each kind of animal, male and female. And bring food to feed all the creatures for many days."

Noah and his sons began to build the ark. Their wives gathered food. Soon the ark was ready. God sent male and female of each kind of bird and animal and creeping thing.

When all the creatures were inside, Noah went into the ark with his family. Then God shut the door of the ark and sealed it. The rain began.

For forty days and forty nights the rain did not stop. The water kept rising, and Noah's ark floated on the waves.

Everything that God had made died. Only Noah and those in the ark were alive.

After forty days and forty nights, the rain stopped and the water went down. The ark came to rest atop a mountain.

Noah sent out a dove to see if the earth was dry. The dove could not find a dry place to land, and it returned to the ark.

Seven days later Noah sent out the dove again. When the dove came back carrying an olive leaf, Noah knew the water still covered all but the highest treetops.

After seven more days, Noah sent out the dove, and it did not come back. It had found a dry place to nest. The earth was dry again.

God told Noah to come out of the ark. Noah, his family, and all the animals stepped out onto dry land.

Noah built an altar to worship God.

God was pleased, and He made a promise to Noah. "I will never again send a flood to kill all the living things on earth," He said. "The rainbow is a sign that I remember this promise for all time."

Joseph and the Coat of Many Colors

Jacob had twelve sons. He loved one son, Joseph, best of all. He gave Joseph a coat of many colors, which made Joseph's brothers jealous.

A short time later Joseph had two dreams foretelling that his father and mother and brothers would bow down before him.

When Joseph told his family about the dreams, his brothers grew more jealous. One day when the brothers were in the fields, they decided to kill Joseph. But the oldest brother said, "Let's throw Joseph into a pit, but let's not kill him."

Joseph's brothers took his many-colored coat and threw him into a deep hole.

Another brother suggested that they sell Joseph to caravan traders, to be a slave.

After the brothers sold Joseph, they took his coat and dipped it into the blood of an animal. When Jacob saw the coat, he thought Joseph had been killed.

In Egypt, Joseph was sold to Potiphar, the captain of the king's guard. Potiphar's wife hated Joseph, and she told lies about him to her husband. Potiphar threw Joseph into prison.

One night the king's cupbearer and his baker, who were in prison, each had a dream. They told their dreams to Joseph, who knew that God would help him understand the dreams. Joseph told them that the baker was to be killed, but the cupbearer would serve the king again.

Just as Joseph had said, the baker was hanged and the cupbearer went to serve the king.

Two years later the king had a dream, and no one could tell him what it meant. Then the cupbearer remembered Joseph.

Joseph told the king that his dream meant there would be seven years of plenty in Egypt, then seven years of famine.

The king put Joseph in charge of the kingdom, to build storehouses for the extra food that would grow during the years of plenty.

For seven years the crops grew well. Then there was famine everywhere. Only in Egypt was there plenty to eat.

There was no food where Jacob and his sons lived. So Jacob sent all but Benjamin, the youngest of his sons, to Egypt to buy food.

In Egypt, Jacob's sons bowed down before Joseph, just as Joseph's dream had foretold.

Joseph recognized his brothers, but they did not recognize him. He asked them about their homeland and their family. Then Joseph said, "You are spies!"

The brothers said that they had come to buy food.

"If you are honest," Joseph said, "one of you will remain here while the rest bring food to your family. Then come back with your youngest brother."

One brother stayed in Egypt while the others returned home. When their food was all gone, Jacob told his sons to return to Egypt to buy more and to take Benjamin with them.

When Joseph saw his brothers, he gave them grain. Then he told his servants to hide a silver cup in Benjamin's sack.

When the brothers left, Joseph sent his servants after them, to accuse them of stealing the cup. Joseph wanted to make his brothers come back.

When his brothers returned, Joseph told them that he was their brother. He asked them to go and bring all of Jacob's family back to Egypt.

"Now you see," he said, "that God sent me here, to save you and all my people from hunger."

Moses in the Bulrushes

The Hebrews lived in Egypt for many years. There they became so numerous that the king feared them and made them slaves.

But the Hebrews continued to prosper. The king commanded that all newborn Hebrew boys be cast into the Nile River and drowned.

One mother hid her baby boy for months. When the baby grew, she placed him in a basket and put the basket into the Nile. The woman asked her daughter to stay and see what would happen to the baby.

When the king's daughter came down to the river to bathe, she saw the basket among the bulrushes. She ordered her servants to bring it to her.

When the princess saw the baby in the basket, she knew he was a Hebrew. But she decided to raise him as her own.

The girl left her hiding place and told the princess that she knew a Hebrew woman who could nurse the child. Then she ran home and brought back her mother.

So the baby was nursed by his own mother, who brought him to the palace when he was older. The princess named the boy Moses, and he was treated as a prince.

One day Moses saw an Egyptian beating a Hebrew. In anger, Moses killed the Egyptian and hid the body in the sand.

The king heard what Moses had done. He was very angry and wanted to kill Moses. So Moses fled.

When the king of Egypt died, a crueler king ruled in his place.

The Israelites cried out to God. God would send Moses to help them.

One day Moses was tending sheep. A blazing fire appeared in the middle of a bush, but the bush did not burn up.

God called to Moses from the bush. "I have seen the sorrow of My people. Go to the king so that you may bring them out of Egypt."

Moses answered, "Why should anyone believe me when I tell them You have sent me?"

God said, "Throw your staff to the ground."

Moses did, and the staff became a serpent. Then he picked it up, and it became a staff again.

God said, "Take that staff with you. And take Aaron, your brother, to help you."

So Moses and Aaron went to the king of Egypt, but the king would not let the Israelites go.

Aaron threw down Moses' staff, and the staff became a serpent. The king ordered his magicians to throw down their staffs. When their staffs turned into serpents, Moses' serpent ate all the others. But the king still would not listen.

Moses went to the king again, but the king still refused to let the Israelites leave Egypt.

So Aaron stretched out his staff over the Nile. The river turned to blood, and the blood flowed for seven days. Still the king would not listen to Moses. So God struck Egypt with other plagues.

First all of Egypt was filled with frogs, then insects, then flies. After that, the cattle died. Then the Egyptians got boils on their skin. God sent hail, then swarms of locusts. Then God sent thick darkness.

At last God sent His final plague: Every firstborn Egyptian child would die.

Moses told each Israelite family to kill a lamb and spread the blood on the doorway of their home. "God will see the blood and pass over the house. But the houses of the Egyptians will not be marked, and He will strike there."

In the homes of the Israelites, the people thanked God for sparing their children.

Among the Egyptians, even the king's son was not spared. The king sent for Moses and said, "Get out from among my people."

So Moses and the Israelites left Egypt. Before long the king sent his army after them. The army caught up with the Israelites on the banks of the Red Sea.

God told Moses to raise his staff over the Red Sea. The waters parted, and the Israelites passed over to the other side.

When the Egyptians tried to follow, God caused the waters to fall back and drown them.

The Israelites thanked God for freeing them from Egypt, and for sending Moses to guide them to their true home.

David and Goliath

There was a war in the land of Israel. The Philistine armies were ready, and King Saul and the men of Israel were ready, too.

A Philistine champion appeared, a giant named Goliath. He cried to the men of Israel, "Choose a champion. If he can kill me, the Philistines will be your servants. But if I kill him, you shall be our servants."

Saul and his men knew they did not have a man who could defeat the giant.

There was a boy named David who was the youngest of eight sons. His older brothers served in the army, but David took care of his father's sheep at home.

One day David's father told David to take some food to his brothers and to bring back news of the war.

David went to find his brothers.

While David talked with his brothers Goliath came out to challenge the army of Israel. When the soldiers saw Goliath, they ran away.

Some men said to David, "King Saul will give riches and his daughter in marriage to the man who can kill the giant."

David said, "Who is this Philistine to threaten the army of the living God?"

When David's words were told to King Saul, he sent for David.

David said, "I will go and fight Goliath."

But Saul said, "You are a boy, and he is a trained soldier."

David said, "While I kept my father's sheep a lion came and took a lamb out of the flock. I killed the lion. This giant shall be like that lion. The Lord will deliver me from Goliath."

Saul said, "Go, and the Lord be with you."

King Saul gave David his own armor to wear in the battle. David was not used to armor, and he gave it back.

David picked up his staff. Then he put five smooth stones in his bag, took his sling, and went out to meet Goliath.

David said, "I come in the name of the Lord. The Lord will deliver you into my hand, that all the earth may know there is a God in Israel."

David put one of his stones in his sling, aimed, and let go. The stone struck the Philistine's forehead, and Goliath fell to the ground.

Then David took Goliath's sword and cut off the giant's head.

When the Philistines saw that their champion was dead, they ran away. The men of Israel chased after them.

So David defeated the Philistines with a sling and a stone, and the help of the living God.

The Lord Is My Shepherd
The Twenty-third Psalm

The Lord is my Shepherd; I shall not want.
He maketh me to lie down in green pastures.
He leadeth me beside the still waters.
He restoreth my soul.
He leadeth me in the paths of righteousness, for His name's sake.
Yea, though I walk through the valley of the shadow of death,
I will fear no evil, for Thou art with me.
Thy rod and Thy staff, they comfort me.
Thou preparest a table before me in the sight of mine enemies.
Thou anointest my head with oil.
My cup runneth over.
Surely goodness and mercy shall follow me all the days of my life,
and I shall dwell in the house of the Lord forever.

The Story of Jonah

The Lord said to Jonah, "Go to Nineveh and tell the people that I have heard of their wickedness. If they do not change their ways, Nineveh will be destroyed."

But Jonah rose up and found a ship bound for another city. He paid his fare and went on board.

The Lord caused a great storm to come up. The sailors were afraid. Each man called on his own god to save him.

Jonah was asleep. The captain said to Jonah, "Get up and call on your god! Perhaps your god will save us."

The sailors rolled dice to see who was to blame for the storm. The blame fell to Jonah.

Then Jonah told them, "My God has brought this storm upon you because of me. Throw me into the sea."

The sailors did not want Jonah to drown. But the storm grew worse.

The men begged Jonah's God for mercy. Then they threw Jonah into the sea.

The sea grew calm, and the sailors prayed to Jonah's God.

The Lord sent a huge fish to swallow Jonah. Jonah was inside the fish for three days and nights. Then Jonah prayed to the Lord. He said, "I will do what I have promised."

The Lord commanded the great fish to cough up Jonah onto dry land.

The Lord said to Jonah, "Go to Nineveh and say what I shall tell you."

Jonah went to Nineveh. He walked through the city, crying, "In forty days, Nineveh will be destroyed."

When the people heard Jonah's words, they believed in the Lord God. The king of Nineveh ordered all his people to stop their wicked ways and pray to the Lord God.

The Lord God did not destroy the city.

And Jonah was angry. He thought his trip to Nineveh had been useless.

Jonah went out of the city and built a shelter.

And the Lord God caused a plant to grow up, to shade Jonah from the heat.

But at dawn the next day, God sent a worm to kill the plant. Then the sun beat down on Jonah. He grew faint and begged God to let him die.

Then God said, "You felt sorry for the plant, which you did not raise or tend, and which lived only for a day and a night.

"Should I not then feel sorry for Nineveh, where there are so many people and animals, all of them My children?"

Daniel in the Lions' Den

When Nebuchadnezzar was king of Babylon, he conquered Israel and captured Jerusalem.

Nebuchadnezzar ordered that a number of Israelite boys be brought back to Babylon. Among them was a boy named Daniel.

The king commanded that the boys be served the best food and wine. But Daniel did not want to eat the king's food, because doing so was against God's law.

The king's officer felt sorry for Daniel, and after that, Daniel did not have to eat the king's food.

God was pleased with Daniel for obeying His law. He gave Daniel wisdom and the ability to understand dreams.

Daniel and three of his friends were chosen to serve the king. The king thought they were wiser than all the wise men in the kingdom.

Nebuchadnezzar had dreams that kept him from sleeping. He sent for his wise men. The king wanted them to tell him what his dreams meant. When they could not, Nebuchadnezzar ordered that all the wise men in the kingdom be killed.

The soldiers went to kill Daniel and his friends as well. But Daniel persuaded them to let him talk with the king.

Daniel told the king, "If you will wait till tomorrow, I will tell you what you dreamed and the meaning of it." Nebuchadnezzar agreed.

Daniel and his friends prayed to God. That night God showed Daniel the king's dream.

The next day Daniel told the king what he had dreamed and what it meant. The king said, "Surely your God is the God of gods, since He caused you to explain this mystery."

Nebuchadnezzar made Daniel governor over Babylon and chief of all the wise men.

When the king had another dream, he sent for Daniel.

Daniel said, "You will be driven away from your people. You will live with animals and eat grass like the cattle. Seven years will pass. Then you will recognize that God rules—even over kings."

One year later all that Daniel had told the king came true.

After seven years had passed, Nebuchadnezzar praised and honored God. Then he became king once more.

When Nebuchadnezzar died, his son, Belshazzar, became king. But Belshazzar did not honor God.

One day Belshazzar gave a banquet. A hand suddenly appeared and began writing on the wall in front of him. None of the guests could read the writing. Belshazzar sent for Daniel.

Daniel told Belshazzar that he had not served God, as his father had learned to do. The writing on the wall said that God had put an end to Belshazzar's kingdom. It had been given to his enemies.

That night Belshazzar was killed, and Darius the Mede became king. Darius appointed Daniel and two other men to govern the kingdom.

Darius found that Daniel was a better governor than the others. He wanted Daniel to govern the kingdom by himself.

That made the other governors angry. They tricked Darius into making a new law: Any person who prayed to anyone but the king would be thrown into a den of lions.

Even though Daniel knew about the law, he continued to pray to God. The other governors told Darius that Daniel had broken the law. They said that Daniel should be thrown into the lions' den.

After Daniel was brought inside the lions' den, a large stone was rolled across the opening to seal him in.

Darius ran to the lions' den and called out to Daniel, "Has your God been able to save you?"

Daniel answered, "My God sent His angels and shut the lions' mouths."

The stone was rolled away from the opening, and Daniel walked out. Darius commanded that the other governors be thrown into the lions' den. He ordered the people of his kingdom to worship the living God of Daniel, who had delivered his servant from the lions.